Praise for the Three Priceless Techniques:

"The Three Priceless Techniques in Daniel's new book are a transformative treasure indeed, as well as wise, accessible and practical—and I use them myself. I delight in what he has done here with his spiritual parable, a perfect fit for our time, place, and troubled world, and recommend it heartily to all those who seek a better life and world for us all." **--Lama Surya Das,** author of *Awakening the Christ Within; Tibetan Wisdom for the Western World,* Founder of the Dzogchen Meditation Center.

"This book is an inspiring and delightful tool for daily practices. It teaches simple Techniques that today's humanity needs to deal with their day-to-day challenges. It is also a great beginning to understand suffering and connect with your inner Christ." **--Sri Madhuji**

"Daniel and Rekha's attempt at transforming higher philosophy into an easily digestible concept with a simple application exercise is indeed commendable! Those involved in modern research of Epigenetics, Quantum Physics and similar approaches, which are changing the dimensions and dynamics of healing and curing, a real-life attempt at imbibing the concepts in Krishna's Kingdom, it would help smooth the journey for the practitioner. Mind over matter comes out very well and what is more in a readable and applicable format." -- **Ramesh Lakshman**, Chartered Accountant and Area Head of Finance at SP Jain School of Global Business

"It was a pleasure reading the novel Krishna's kingdom by Daniel O' Hara and Rekha Balaji. It is well written and contains sound, practical advice. We see so much of negativity in life and this is so refreshing to have a positive, upbeat through this novel's Three Priceless Techniques. The story is a blend of fiction and reality. It is so intricately woven that there is a hairline difference. The story lends to educating to educating the society and making complex situations to handle, so simple. The authors have explicitly brought out the techniques to handle life in a better way with a broader perspective." -- **Ruth Brewart,** Academic Co-Ordinator

Velammal Newgen School, Surapet

"Daniel, what a phenomenal book! I so enjoyed the story and the teachings. The Three Priceless Techniques that you describe (and show how to use in our everyday lives) are so powerful that I am incorporating them into my own practice. What a gift you have written for humanity, as it will change how people look at themselves and the world. You will know you are different and transformed from the minute you wake up in the morning. Thank you, thank you!!!"
--Dr. Eric Robins, co-author of *Your Hands Can Heal You*

"Daniel O'Hara brings joy, inspiration and uniqueness to this spiritual journey of wisdom that will touch, heal and uplift the young and old alike. A must read!"
--Kim Somers Egelsee, #1 best-selling author of *Getting Your Life to a 10+*

"Daniel's Christ Castles is such a relatable story. An investment of an hour will pay dividends for the rest of your life!" **--Loren Slocum, CEO** of Lobella Int'l and author of *Life Tune-ups: Your Personal Plan to Find Balance, Discover Your Passion, and Step into Greatness*

"Daniel has written an "old soul" book. It's full of ancient wisdom, but it's exceptionally applicable in the modern world. It's evolved, practical and easy-to-use." **--John Merryman,** co-author of *Your Hands Can Heal You*

"There's a volcano's worth of energy, power, light, and transformation inside this little book!" **--Karen Rauch Carter,** author of *Move Your Stuff, Change Your Life* and *Make a Shift, Change Your Life*

"Daniel O'Hara brings practical Buddhism to daily life in his new book, 'Christ Castles.' In simple parable form, he teaches us how to improve our lives and the lives of those around us without excessive words and practices. Daniel is a master spiritual teacher of the obscured by gently and effectively opening our eyes to the obvious. A great read for anyone and everyone." **--Tom Zender,** President Emeritus of Unity

Krishna's Kingdom: Three Priceless Techniques to Transform Your Life!

(Book One in the Krishna's Kingdom Series)

By Daniel O'Hara and Rekha Balaji

Copyright © 2017 by Daniel O'Hara and Rekha Balaji

This book and other titles and videos can be found at:

www.DanielOHara.com

Printed in the U.S.A

KRISHNA'S KINGDOM

Three Priceless Techniques
To Transform Your Life!

(Book One in the
Krishna's Kingdom Series)

by

Daniel O'Hara and Rekha Balaji

PURPOSE:

This book was written for anyone, whether Hindu or even an atheist, who would like to have a better life.

I hope you enjoy this most relatable, entertaining story; and more importantly, that you will apply these **Three Priceless Techniques.** They will help you to effortlessly free yourself of limiting beliefs, negative emotional states, and transform every area of your life!

You can easily read this book in under two hours. Some readers choose to read it a little bit at a time. Most readers re-read it many times, as there tends to be an *experience* each time. Many are calling **Krishna's Kingdom** - *The Experience Book.*

The Crisis

My hands were trembling... My head was pounding as if Mary Kom was continually beating on it. With each punch came more damage and trauma. While earlier in the day I had delivered the presentation of my life, and literally wowed the conference room; this simply didn't matter anymore. One of the greatest achievements in my career was now a distant memory. I was overwhelmed with a huge predicament and didn't know how to get out of it. My evening had turned into a nightmare...

The day started off great and festivities were planned for the evening. Rashmi and I were celebrating our tenth wedding anniversary along with our son Ayaan's eighth birthday. The house felt airy, festive and joy-filled. There was a special indescribable happiness- a palpable feeling of benevolence.

At work, I delivered the presentation of my life. It was in front of the Board, the Executive Leadership team and most of the company. The CEO/President of the company, my biggest fan, loved it! My team loved it! My direct superior however, did not! The attention I received from the CEO/President brought out the dark side of my direct superior, Raghu. Raghu, while overall a good guy, still had some character flaws. Most of my co-workers loved it; however, there were still some that took it as a personal threat to their positions. Tonight, none of these workplace events mattered. It was all about our son.

It was 5:30 PM, and my life had suddenly become *surreal.* We were preparing for our anniversary and Ayaan's birthday celebrations for the evening. I was getting ready to leave, so I could watch the end of Ayaan's football practice; when I received a call on my cell from a number I didn't recognize. Still buzzing in preparation for the night at hand and post-bliss of the events of the day, I cheerfully answered.

After a quick obligatory "Hello," the caller frantically attempted to put words together. It was Ayaan's coach. As the coach blurted, "The ambulance is on its way," these words made the one hundred trillion cells in my body tremble with concern for my progeny. I had great difficulty trying to come up with words to respond and doled out, "Huh?" Regaining my senses, I immediately queried, "What…What happened?"

The coach proceeded to explain that Ayaan was making a tackle, and he incorrectly put his head down resulting in a concussion. He was now unconscious. The ambulance and paramedics had just arrived. They were examining him now. I was to meet them at the hospital. I was immediately propelled into a mental and emotional fog. I felt as if I was floating on a small boat in the middle of the ocean with no clue as to the whereabouts of land and/or direction. It was so *surreal.*

Entering the emergency room doors, my body was now fueled with adrenaline. This fuel gave me the energy to cope with the current situation but helped to inflame the tension in my neck and shoulders. Mentally, I was unclear, and my emotions were a cocktail of uncertainty- two-parts concern and one-part hope that everything would be okay. Once through security I found hallways of people in a world of organized chaos. Ayaan's room was the last door at the end of the longest hall. There was a small gaggle of nurses and doctors examining him. After maybe fifteen minutes (of what seemed like hours), from what I could gather from their conversation, they were going to do more evaluations including a CAT Scan, an MRI and an overnight stay for observation.

Ayaan was soon *gurnied* to another room that was even more impersonal and almost vault-like. Through a small window, I could see Ayaan from a distance. Watching him through a looking glass in the waiting room made me feel more like a distant observer than a concerned parent. The CAT Scan machine entwined Ayaan like a giant, metallic cobra grasping her body and swallowing her head.

Was this whole experience *real*, a dream or rather, just a nightmare? "If it was just a nightmare, PLEASE, wake me up," I mentally pleaded. Or, worse yet, was this some sort of punishment? I'd never really done anything bad in my life, or at least so I thought. When I was young, I was a self-absorbed idiot and I acted like most kids during my teenage years – unaware and with selfish intentions. While I wasn't a saint by any stretch, I certainly never tried to hurt other people. This internal dialogue was circling in my head from the adrenaline dump. As the adrenaline started wearing off, my body told my mind it needed a chair, so I sat down.

My physical body was tired, my brain still continued thinking, albeit at a slower pace, on its own. Perhaps it was the last bits of adrenaline hitting the cerebral cortex. "Was our son going to be OK? Was he going to have brain damage? Was he going to be paralyzed? Was he ever going to be the same strong, fun loving kid?" were questions that revealed themselves due to the fragile nature of the situation at hand.

"Surely, there was a better way?" I thought. My thoughts continued, "Was there some sort of moksha to this suffering? Oh God, please help!" I thought, almost screaming in my mind… "Please help! There must be a better way of living my life without all this suffering. I'm so tired of the pain and the pain I see in the world." While today was extraordinary, most days were a struggle, and tonight was just too much to bear.

This inner dialogue of requesting help, surrender or whatever it was called; was very foreign to me. While sitting, or rather due to my tiredness, now reclining uncomfortably in the hospital chair, I closed my eyes and started drifting off to sleep…

The Dream

Most nights it took time to fall asleep. I often resorted to drowning a peg of scotch, reading a book, or ingesting an over-the-counter sleeping pill for any hope of rapid slumber. I was one of the 48% of people in America who suffered from insomnia. Needing something external to help me fall asleep and to break the monotonous routine of lying sleepless, I would sometimes add one of those *plop, plop, fizz, fizz* things to a glass of water. It was also supposed to help with sinuses, which also bothered me. I believed, "Why not accomplish both?"

Watching the white wafer hit the water was like watching a mini-explosion with an accompanying fizz sound. While it didn't completely knock me out, it was good for a little bit of tension relief. The commercial used to chime "Oh, what a relief it is…," and this jingle played in my head each time. Tonight, for a change, an external aid, or bedtime ritual wasn't needed. The roller coaster of emotional highs and lows of the day had finally fatigued my poor body and mind. This fatigue created an easy transition from waking consciousness to sleep.

Unaware that I was now sleeping, I found myself in a dream. While awake, the physical world seemed *real.* However, this dream world seemed to be even more *real.* "How could this be even more *real*?" I thought.

From the darkness, a golden orb of light appeared, moving ever closer into my awareness. Its emergence from total darkness jolted my already *realer* feeling to an even more intensified state.

The bright orb now visible to my closed, *inner* eyes morphed into the Krishna. In this particular dream, the colors were more vibrant and the sensations were more experiential. "Rohan," the Krishna said as he sat leaning next to me, "The life you wished for when you fell asleep *is possible; it does exist!*"

I was clearly hearing the words of the Krishna speaking to me, as if it was *realer* than a conversation with another human. "What in the world?" I deliberated.

The Krishna continued, "While you think this physical world you live in is real, it is merely an illusion. It is all Maya within your mind…"

Never having a frame of reference for such an experience, I was wondering what was happening. This was the first time I had ever had such a vivid and real encounter or let alone a dream like this before. I immediately asked, "Why are you here?" Before providing the Krishna an opportunity to respond, I continued and blurted out, "Why are you helping *me?*"

The Krishna smiled. With a grace and tone unlike any other, he shared, "Because, you asked." He said he was moved by my deep desire to get out of misery, and his compassionate nature allowed him to intervene when genuine cries for help warranted it. "Rohan, you have the ability to get out of suffering."

I now paused for a moment, a rarity for me, and took in what he said. As if he was reading my mind, I was wondering if I could ever get out of this hamster wheel of pain, pleasure, and only to be followed up with more anguish.

"The problem is with your over identification of the transient world around you, Rohan. You believe your world is real. In the Bhagavad Gita I have said that the world you see with your physical eyes, the world of my illusion is called *Maya*. Our world is not an objective one; rather, it's subjective, pliant, and endlessly mutable. In other words, our senses, the very means by which we gather data about the world, are unreliable because they are prone to illusion. They don't give us direct access to an objective world; rather, they give an illusion of objectivity as explained in Chapter 7, verse 14:

daivī hyeṣhā guṇa-mayī mama māyā duratyayā
mām eva ye prapadyante māyām etāṁ taranti te

Ordinary people are unable to escape from the spell of this cosmic hypnosis (maya) as they are deluded by the material modes of ignorance, passion, and goodness. These three modes of Maya veil their consciousness and as a result, they become fascinated by ephemeral allurement of bodily pleasures. The material world is very real, but, like a house of mirrors, its purpose is to delude us. Similarly, the physical world is real, you and I are real, but like the mirrors in a fun house, our material senses distort our perceptions.

In this dream, I sensed something inside me was changing. My body felt less heavy, a lightening of sorts was occurring. For much of my life, I had always felt reactive and defensive. There had been many times that my life was filled with high hopes of a glorious outcome, whether it be financial, work-related, or with my home-life; only to have something bad occur at the last minute. The last *eleventh hour* of disappointments sent my emotions spiraling out of control only to be followed by a crash landing. Needless to say, I usually reacted harshly, negatively, and self-destructively after these setbacks.

This internal feeling of *lightness* was gaining momentum, as I started feeling yet another round of improvement. Rather than feeling my standard defensive and guarded response, which made me feel heavy and congested; I was now feeling an ability to be proactive. This feeling of being proactive gave me hope that I might be able to create the reality with which the Krishna was so eloquently speaking. In some indiscernible way, I intuitively knew what was happening... His gracious presence initiated a *domino effect* that let me see my life from a different perspective, and that my physical illusion *was* changing. I felt I had a better handle on this whole experience. "Of course, this whole thing was a dream, and maybe I was just deluding myself," I inwardly chuckled to myself. If I was chuckling during this time of crisis, maybe this whole dream was *real* after all?!

He remained sitting there patiently looking at me, so I decided to ask another question, "How can I change it - this *Maya* thing- the illusion I mean?"

The Krishna smiled and said, "Rohan, it is really very easy! I will teach you **Three Priceless Techniques.** The more you apply these **Techniques** in your daily life, the easier they will become, and the less stressful your life will be. Your life will have much more peace, meaning, ease, and you'll help those around you, as well."

I was dubious, but captivated. "I really had the power to change myself and those who surround me? And, with only **Three Techniques?**" I mulled over to myself and I wanted to hear more. Yet, a part of me was still feeling reluctant to change, and I was still skeptical. While the way I lived my life was probably killing me at an ever-accelerated rate, it was my routine. It was all I knew, and I had never been very good at adopting new routines.

The Krishna continued, "Not only will these **Techniques** help you and your life, but these **Techniques** will help magnetize others to do the same. As more people do them, you and others will have the power to transform the world into a giant *Krishna's Kingdom.*"

"Krishna's Kingdom... What is a *Krishna's Kingdom?"* I asked.

"Good question," the pleased Krishna replied. "I'll explain that in a moment. But first, in order for you to understand where you are going, we need to review where you've been!"

The Review

With a whoosh, the Krishna and I seemed to be reclining on a hammock in an imaginary lush green courtyard overlooking a beautiful garden. From this *Krishna Courtyard perspective*, we looked down and saw my bedroom with my sleeping body in bed.

It was a Monday morning and a little after sunrise. I watched as I slammed the off button on my digital alarm clock, a bit harder than intended, and the clock slid a few inches on the nightstand. We watched my head fall back onto my pillow and my eyes close again. I drew in a quick, somewhat tense breath and appeared to brace myself for the new day. I watched myself attempting to get out of bed. I didn't look happy. The king-sized bed was empty on the other side. Rashmi had been up long enough that her side was cold.

Monday mornings seemed to worsen with the sound of an electronic, buzzing alarm clock that somehow never troubled Rashmi. "Why do companies make clocks with such irritating alarms? Why start the day off irritated?" I deliberated to myself. "One of these days I should get an alarm connected to my iPhone and play the famous play U2's *Beautiful Day* upon waking. At least, that song would inspire happy thoughts and set a much better tone for the day." I wondered if I was the only one to think such thoughts, as I watched my body slowly roll out of bed. With heavy feet and sleepy guck in my eyes, my body lumbered to the bathroom.

I was slightly sad watching this daily ritual of waking, and I looked to the Krishna for comfort and guidance. Not changing his facial expression in any way, his gentle smile oozed with peace, and that smile gave me some modicum of reassurance of a better life.

My entry into the shower marked my favorite part of each morning. Three to five minutes of peace before the mundane drudgery and conflict in my daily life would begin. There was something delightful about the caress of the water upon my skin that not only washed off my body, but also seemed to revitalize and nurture my soul - whatever that meant . . .

Perhaps it simply felt good to do something that was directed purely for my rejuvenation. "Maybe it was the comfort of a morning ritual, like a knight donning his armor? Whatever it was, I told myself that I was better not to over-analyze it and ruin the moment because the moment was feeling good," I counseled myself. I rationalized that too much thinking was like playing your favorite album too many times. Over the years, I annoyed my family on many occasions by playing a song over and over again. Maybe I should stop replaying thoughts in my head and irritating myself, as well.

The Krishna looked at me watching this shower scene play out without saying anything, yet his look appeared to confirm that my shower dialogue was right.

"Wow," I thought, "I'm conversing with a Krishna in a dream and watching myself in a shower. And, while I'm in the

shower, I'm thinking, and now the Krishna is complimenting me...
Whoa... There are a lot of levels to this. I have a lot to learn," I
reflected to myself. As these new realizations revealed themselves,
my jaw was starting to relax, and a warm smile emerged, as I stood
on the *Krishna Courtyard.*

Emerging from the shower, a fragment of a scene played in
my mind's eye. It was an image from the same elusive dream that
I had been having over years. I felt peaceful, saw something
golden, and then poof it was gone!

I exchanged a few brief words with my wife Rashmi about
her plans for the day. Between getting herself ready each morning,
cooking meals and getting the kids rushed off to school, the
conversation was always hasty and incomplete. Most of the time,
she was rushing around hurriedly. With her attention in many
directions, I was challenged in hearing her words correctly. This
inability to hear her clearly aggravated me to no end. It seemed
that she always turned her head away from me on the key word in
a sentence. Not hearing that key word allowed for several
interpretations in her sentence. While many husbands might not
have cared about what their wife had to say, I cared what she had
to say. I wished that she was more composed, relaxed, and was
able to look at me when she was speaking. Maybe, it was too
much to ask given all of her responsibilities with the kids, home
and work? I remembered a bumper sticker I once saw, *The best
gift you can give someone is your presence.*

Conversations with Rashmi were more productive and
harmonious later in the evening, after nine to be more specific.

Although we were both tired at the end of the day, at least we weren't rushing around, and could speak in the same room without anyone else vying for our attention. I looked forward to these less intense moments, but it seemed that those times were growing fewer with each passing year.

This time when I looked over at the Krishna, I was embarrassed by my aggravation with Rashmi. She was so busy, and who was I to judge her? I certainly wasn't perfect. And besides, to be aggravated by her working so hard for our family was really pretty immature, I realized.

The Krishna maintained his smile as if to say, "Very good!" The Krishna showed me these scenes as if we were watching a movie together. I was the lead character in this drama. A drama it was, and there was way too much drama!

A drama that proved pretty saddening. Watching myself as a spectator helped me a great deal. I was more detached as I witnessed myself entangled in the barbed tentacles of my own emotions, thoughts and beliefs. These tentacles were like squid drowning me. I remembered a show National Geographic that I watched about the Colossal Squid, and how their tentacles had suckers with rotating hooks inside them. Their arms would hold their victim, the rotating hooks which were inside the suckers, would slice the flesh and move into meat to the squid's beak. Recalling the rotating hooks made my *mental movie* even scarier. I started reflecting on how poorly I started off my day, and more importantly, how many flaws I had. I now saw these flaws as hooks.

Again, without changing his demeanor or expression the Krishna gave me his consistent smile of support. I sensed his confirmation that I was finally getting it, and we quickly transitioned to the next part of the day.

We moved to a scene at the breakfast table. From the *Krishna Courtyard* I watched as I munched sullenly on my breakfast. The brown bread *(roti)* seemed like a metaphor for the tone of my day, nothing but life depleting brown... As I read the paper, I saw nothing but conflicts. Murders, military skirmishes, children developing autism, crooked politicians, GMOs in our food supply, and a local company CEO caught lying to its shareholders filled the pages. "Where was there not suffering in the world," I quixotically reflected.

In the background, our kids were starting off the day with their own mini-version of global conflict; fighting over the cable remote control.

"I want to watch Spiderman!" yelled my son Ayaan. "NO! I want to watch Dora!" shouted Diya, the younger of the two.

From my position on the sidelines, I saw how, even in the early stages of childhood, there seemed to be an inherent tendency towards conflict. And, it appeared from reading the paper, it only progressed and worsened as we become adults, I surmised.

It was *surreal* to be with the Krishna, again watching myself experience *my* day. While watching my review, I was able to feel the stress of the day and hear my own internal dialogue. The most beneficial part was examining these very thoughts, emotions and encounters with the enlightening presence of the Krishna. Having him *over my shoulder* watching my reactions to these scenes helped me improve my awareness. I surveyed many blocks on my road of life. Some of the blocks were like giant boulders, lodged in potholes on my highway to becoming a better person.

The Review of the Drive

While going to work and probably likely for most people, I habitually found the transition from our home to my car somewhat depressing. It was as if I was compartmentalizing from our humble home into a smaller metal box of a vehicle. From one box providing my body a place to rest to a smaller box that provided my body transportation. Once at work I would further compartmentalize again into a cubicle. I was fortunate that I had worked my way up to own office, which made the whole *compartmentalizing* process a little more palatable.

As I pulled out of the driveway, the car stereo came on with two local DJs, who made the tedious drive to work a little more bearable. I listened to their show every morning during the workweek. I noticed a pattern in their intention to laugh approximately every 22 seconds. Counting to 22 and listening for their conjured laughter actually made me chuckle. The topics of their jokes consisted of the usual: men, women, body parts, relationships, bosses, current news, celebrities, and of course the easiest and best target, politicians.

Making my way through rush hour traffic on the highway, I wondered how long it would take for another car to cut me off. The drive on the 405 freeway each morning was no treat. I could get to my office in only fifteen minutes if it wasn't for the traffic, but instead it usually took 45-50 minutes.

Slamming my right foot onto the brake, the event I anticipated suddenly occurred. Being cutoff in traffic was almost similar to the consistency of fake laughter by the morning DJs. Another driver in a new Porsche cut me off. He would have hit my car had it not been for my anticipation of his actions and having decent reflexes. The rude driver raised his hand in the air at me while looking in his rear-view mirror, as if to say I was at fault. The audacity of him blaming me granted me the license to fly off the handle in retort. So, I mouthed clearly, "You're an asshole!" so that he could read my lips while he was looking back at me.

I remembered reading about two guys yelling at each other on the freeway, and it resulted in a shooting and a death. The news was filled with events like this. I thought this was so pointless. Fighting over inconsequential space on a freeway was moronic. My heart was racing after this experience, and my body grew tenser. The day was still so young, and I was already beginning to feel old and tired . . . "If I felt this way at only 35," I said to myself, "How old would I feel like when I was 45 or 55?" I thought to myself.

I looked over at the Krishna. By just turning and looking to him, I didn't need to say anything. It was clear - I acted like an ass. Who was I to be so negative to people? And, what a waste of energy! It started becoming clear to me. I was directing negative energy at this random guy on the highway. In fact, while I re-watched this scene again, for a microsecond, I thought I saw red energy being hurled back and forth. We were throwing prickly fireballs at each other, and they were hitting our heads, hearts and solar plexus. I started questioning, "Maybe the other guy had so much on his mind that he didn't mean to cut me off? What if I truly wasn't giving him enough space on the freeway? Maybe, he just lost his job, his girlfriend, or something even worse?" I now felt sorry for the poor guy and even more disappointed in myself for being so ignorant.

The Krishna and I had reviewed my morning thus far from the start at home then to the drive to work. Having done this twice now, I was starting to see a pattern emerge. I certainly wasn't proud of what I saw. My emotions and thoughts had continued to escalate with each situation. I would find fault in others and

Continually made myself right. It was like the kindling of an inner fire. These increasingly negative emotions were the sparks that ignited the kindling of my negative thoughts. When combined they would explode into an out-of-control inferno. This inferno would then be projected at others. "Maybe, this type of behavior would lead me one day to *Dante's Inferno*," I pondered.

Maybe to bring myself solace, or out of concern for the well-being of others, I started to wonder if others felt this way too? Surely, I wasn't the only one… We continued into another review session.

The Review of Work

Arriving at the office five minutes late only intensified the stress and duress of my morning. Clocking in on my computer always bothered me. It felt like the company was attaching a shackle to my leg. In a way it was like a physical shackle, as if I was tethered to my desk. It definitely was a mental shackle, since the company owned my mental productivity during business hours. I took pride in doing my job well and maximizing my time. It felt uncomfortable logging in late, even though it was only a few minutes. Or, maybe it was just nagging memories of my mother reminding me to be early. Either way, being late only elevated my stress.

I looked over at the Krishna. While he always maintained his countenance, I sensed he acknowledged what I was thinking. As I watched the scenes playout, I could feel the stresses as an unholy cocktail of chemicals being distributed in my veins. It was early in the day and I was already on my third cup of coffee to keep my energy level up. Despite the Krishna watching my flawed habits, he was still smiling. Although he didn't physically move his eyes or lips, I could swear he squinted his eyes and smiled with pride that I was understanding this deeper way of connecting my experiences.

As the National Director of Sales and marketing, I needed to be a great example to my team. The product managers, who reported to me were already clamoring for my attention and asking questions. I found it particularly annoying when they repeatedly asked the same questions. My facial expressions were probably evident of my thinking that they should know the answer, and I would get exasperated.

One of my sales managers, Sarina Pandey, was quite the character. She had more frenetic energy than anyone I had ever met. While she only drank a cup of coffee in the morning, it seemed like she had five or six shots of espresso. Not having spent much time with people that did drugs regularly, I wondered if she had a drug problem. She was a relatively attractive brunette in her early 40's, and she could talk a mile a minute. Literally, if her mouth was timed, it could compete against the speed of a hummingbird's wings.

She would listen to my advice for about an hour, and then go back to her unproductive work habits of emailing prospective clients instead of calling them. "Had technology moved us beyond our personal relationships and exclusively to digital communication?" I wondered for a moment. Actually, in this case, it was just her fear of not being good enough to engage client initiations over the phone. I had often observed that fear was a major destroyer of capable sales personnel. And, probably not just sales managers, with people in all aspects of life.

Later in the day, I had to attend a steering committee meeting headed by the company's Vice President, Jackson Jones. Jackson had a short, stocky build. For the most part, he was a pretty good guy, except he had a Napoleon complex that overtook his goodness. He wanted everyone to know he was the boss, so much so, that he wanted all of us to call him Mr. Jones. He liked the sound of that, especially since our job was to make him more money.

His primary motivation was furthering his reputation with the CEO/President. He even said and maybe it was a Freudian slip, "He didn't have any friends because all he did was work." All of his interactions with us were centered around his talking about how close he was to the CEO. Since, we weren't his friends - we were all just Jackson's subjects.

My position as National Director of Sales and Marketing was challenging. I was always torn between trying to do what was right for my product managers, the company, and me. I often felt like a juggler with three balls to keep in the air. Having only two hands and no training in juggling, this regularly left a ball falling to the floor. There was, of course, a fourth ball, the clients. My family wasn't even considered in this part of the equation, adding ball number five. And, of course, this resulted in more balls succumbing to the gravity of the earth.

After seeing my pattern of judging someone else, then getting irritated over the interaction, and fueling it with a downward spiral of negative emotions; I once again looked over to the Krishna. This time I smiled at him as if to say, "I get it." My internal process of feeling *lighter* was gaining momentum, and I was feeling hopeful.

While at the meeting, I watched my body rocking back and forth. As my body moved, the chair squeaked, revealing my desire and readiness to leave. And…we were just at the beginning of the meeting. Fortunately for me, this weekly steering committee meeting went rather quickly with little interaction between the attendees- *Jackson's subjects.* While I'm certain Jackson cared for us individually, he cared more about us *collectively.* His management style was more dictatorial. He wanted things done his way, and if you came up with a great idea; his CEO would hear about it as Jackson's idea. The other product managers were uninspired by Jackson's guidance, and the direction he was yet again taking the company.

I sat morosely in my chair as good ole Julie Perez began to shower Jackson with profuse compliments and use words like "brilliant" and "incredible!" Julie was a fiery, Mexican woman. I began to think, that if she had kids, maybe it would have softened her stone-cold heart and ruthless ways. Her business life was all that she had. Whereas, all Jackson cared about was what the CEO thought, Julie was on her own personal quest for power. She would do whatever it took to succeed. We used to joke around that she would even resort to black magic if it would help her career. While she would *brown nose* Jackson in the meetings and effuse him with compliments, she would complain about him behind his back. I always wondered if she was complaining in order to fit in and was conning us just like she conned Jackson.

At nearly every meeting, Julie would rush into the room to stake out her claim. She would sit next to Jackson. Surely, her kissing up would be obvious to Jackson; however, he never seemed to tire of it, or catch on for that matter. He appeared only to revel in it. He preferred hearing the ideas of women, rather than mine or the other men on the team. It appeared that his Napoleonic complex liked the attention of women and thwarted off any male competition.

I was one of the strongest players on the team and carried respect from the group - he especially didn't care for my input. In previous meetings when I had offered input, it was quickly shot down. Once in a while, he'd offer me a flippant compliment on my idea, but it never really seemed sincere or go anywhere. While it was clear to everyone that the CEO believed in me and really treasured me, I hadn't felt support in many years from Jackson. I had served the company for nearly a dozen years, and Jackson seemed to turn my successes into his own. Worse, over time, he just took me for granted. And, as far as promotions go, that was never going to happen…

"Maybe, the problem with Jackson and I was primarily with me," I thought to myself. "Maybe it was predominantly my fault? I started thinking if the problem was just with me than there wouldn't have been problems with Jackson and others. I did a quick review over the dozen years. Many others had left the company as they felt taken advantage of by Jackson. Despite the fact, they wanted to work hard for the company, they felt used by Jackson to advance his career and left, as well. Since, I was one of the original members of management, and one of the last still surviving; the source of the problem was clearly *Jackson.* Too many have left, having their blood, sweat and tears poured in to their territories only to be stolen by Jackson. Jackson was clearly the problem.

As the meeting concluded, Jackson asked me to stay behind in the conference room. One of our clients had complained about one of my sales managers, and it was my job to smooth the situation over. I was to call the client, be apologetic, calm the situation down, and afterward apply the appropriate discipline to the product manager. This whole process was taking a toll on me. It was as if I was like a tank of fuel, and these little quarrels poked a tiny hole in my gas tank. The gas was trickling out, slowly dripping out at first and later leaking more and more. Watching my body walk out of the meeting, my gait was considerably slower. I dreaded these talks with my reps. I was akin to babysitting them on a daily basis.

While I watched the scenes with the Krishna by my side, there may have been some merit to my opinions of co-workers, but I was clearly I was judging them. I judged Jackson on his Napoleonic complex and judged Julie as a power hungry, evil witch. And, while she might have even engaged in *black magic* to advance her career, I was directing negative energy to her just by seeing her in this way. The sad part is, Jackson, or as we were supposed to refer to him, Mr. Jones and I *could* have been great friends had there not been such a pedestal between us.

As I watched myself leave the office and head back to my car, it was clear I was readying myself for the ride home. Just as I closed my door and turned my car on, my cell phone rang. Abruptly, I fumbled around trying to get my earphone in my ear, while simultaneously trying to swipe my card to open the parking garage gate. Doing these three things at once was a recipe for failure. It intensified the feelings of my life being out of control.

As I was taking too long in my exit out of the parking garage, I heard a honk from one of the cars behind me. Getting out of the garage at 5:05 PM was a competitive sport.

Finally, with my earphone successfully in, I was able to address the call. It was my mom calling with something that was very important in *her* world. While major to her, it was an activity that didn't need to be addressed for another month. I quickly closed down the conversation and commenced my way to the busy on-ramp. I looked over at the Krishna with chagrin on my face at the heartlessness I had just displayed to my mom. While it was certainly no excuse, it seemed that people like myself who tried to be nice to people, weren't necessarily the nicest to the people that were closest to them. This infinite revelation was shown in the eyes of the smiling Krishna as if to say, "You are learning a great deal, and we'll cover this topic in the future…"

The Review of the Supermarket

The drive home after work was a repeat of the morning. As usual, I was cut off a couple of times. I, however, was just too tired to give much of a response in these instances. It appeared that this time my tiredness left me apathetic, which was probably better than hostile and warring. The gas out of my imaginary *gas tank* was leaking even more now.

I was making record time on my drive home and was only about four minutes away. I smiled, just a little, thinking I'm almost there; until my cell phone rang again. It was my wife Rashmi, asking me to pick up donuts for our daughter's school function in the morning. Irritated at the request, I quickly and haughtily agreed. My mind was flooded with "Why didn't she do this during day," "She could have easily have done it," and "She knows the store way better than I do." From the *Krishna Courtyard* I watched myself having this imaginary conversation with her, and I could see dark energetic squiggles and patterns forming around my head.

I, continued on with my mental chatter saying "It is going to take forever to find the donuts. The store is going to be ridiculously crowded," and "I'm going to miss the kickoff!" I thought I'd surely miss the first few minutes of *Monday Night Football*, which was a bright spot in my otherwise dull week. The classic *Monday Night Football Theme Song* reminded me of my deceased father, and it was always good for a few endorphins.

At the store, I tried to call her unsuccessfully. "Why is it that cell phones will work in parking structures, even elevators, but not this supermarket?" I agonizingly questioned. I again used my logic to exacerbate my negative emotional state. I could feel my temples tighten and my ears get warm, as my blood-pressure elevated. My visualization of not being able to find the donuts was correct, I had tried quite a few isles without any success.

From the perspective on the *Krishna Courtyard,* I quickly considered that maybe my *visualizations* were creating my negative reality. With a whoosh, I was back watching the scene, not needing confirmation or a reply from the Krishna this time. I was learning at a quicker pace now.

Since I couldn't find the donuts on my own, I needed to find a box-boy or a clerk. It took another five minutes to find a clerk. This was their busiest time of the day, and they were helping people at the checkout stands and not in the aisles. The clerk, whose name was Bob, was a kid. He had just started working there, and he apologized for not knowing where the donuts were either. This did little to comfort my elevated heart rate, the tightness that formed in my temples and shoulders, and the irritation in my abdominal region.

Returning to the front of the store, I asked one of the cashiers for the location of the donuts. As Murphy's Law would have it, the cashier directed me back again to the back of the store. Apparently, the donuts were on the bottom shelves at the end of aisle four. As I walked yet again to the back, my neck tightened, my pulse rate edged up higher, and I weighing the decision on which brand of donuts to buy. Also, what type? This was a stressful dilemma.

I made decisions all day long at work. Yet, was I really stressing over which donuts to purchase? "How ridiculous," I thought. "What the hell..," I barely audibly murmured. Since my cell didn't work in this particular building, and I couldn't ask Rashmi, so I was forced to decide. For a moment, my mind was visualizing that the football game had started, and I was probably missing some great play. It seemed that on this day, all of my decisions were bound to be second-guessed by someone anyway. Why should this donut purchase be any different?

I thought the price for the name-brand donuts were way too high. I wondered why anyone would pay so much for sugar and dough. Instead, I chose several boxes of a generic brand, and quickly headed back up to the checkout line.

All of the lines were overflowing with customers and their carts. Looking for the express line, I staked out my place in line. I noticed a lady in front of me who had approximately 25 items in her cart. The sign clearly read "10 Items or less." She shot me a provoking glance. She seemed to know what I was thinking. It was an *ice-cold glare,* or maybe what in some cultures would be called, an *evil eye.* It was as if she was daring me to say something about it. I thought to myself, "Seriously? You are staring me down, so you can be in front me over donuts? What a day..." I was just too tired to get into any more clashes for the day, and just waited my turn in line. She had emerged victorious in our mental joust.

I did, however, wonder if anyone was observing this lady's indiscretion. I looked around and noticed a supervisor giving instructions to the cashier. It appeared she was just like the clerk I had run into earlier- she was also new. The cashier wasn't yet aware of all the store's procedures and was still learning. I recalled something from the news about a grocery store workers' labor strike, which explained why the lines were extra-long. These workers were just trying to do their new jobs and provide for their families. From the body language of the people waiting in line, the fact that these clerks were new wouldn't be factored into their communications with the newbies.

As I stood in line, going nowhere fast and trying to ignore the lady in front of me, my eyes landed on a magazine cover. Two gorgeous thirty-something movie stars smiled radiantly from the cover. "What perfect lives they must have?" I ruminated. They were super-rich, able to eat at the finest restaurants, travel the world, have adoring fans, and they definitely didn't have to do their own shopping, I hypothesized. I started to fantasize about having their life. For a moment, I even started smiling and felt a little relief in my temples, but then the person behind me suddenly bumped into my back with his cart. To my dismay, the fantasy was abruptly halted… Making things even worse, I had a slight respite from the drudgery with this glimpse of what my life could be like. And now, this fantasy was abruptly taken away nearly as fast as it started.

I knew that my life, by most standards was pretty good. Fantasizing about what my life could have been might leave me even more depressed anyway. I wasn't a rich movie star, and there was no point in pretending that I was; or that having their life was any better than mine. The *evil eye* lady with twenty-five items had finally paid the cashier, and my purchase was the only smooth event of this scene. I was back in my car and soon to be home.

I again turned my head looking at the ever-patient Krishna. He was watching me review the scene at the supermarket. He could see that I was getting it. I was quickly seeing the errors in my interactions with others. He had alluded to a solution to my problems, I was looking forward to the learning of the solutions to my many problems.

Watching the review of my day and this supermarket scene was like eating bad frosting on a scrumptious mud cake. I had a long list of issues that needed to be overcome. Part of me felt like I was being dragged through the proverbial mud, and this review only *one* day of my life. Was I like this all the time? Were my emotions this out of control? In a split second, we were back on the *Krishna Courtyard* watching a new scene.

The Review of Home

Entering our home, I found everything was just as it was when I had left- there was still conflict and chaos. The kids were arguing with each other, and Rashmi was a bit frazzled. She was more exasperated with the kids than anything else, and this was fatiguing for her. She was, however, grateful that I had picked up the donuts. That gratitude lasted for a brief moment until she opened the bag.

When she saw that I had bought generic donuts and not the fancy name brand, Rashmi became heated. She probably had bottled up all of any negative emotions from her day. Dealing with her co-workers, her boss, people at the kid's school, and these emotions were like a powder keg ready to explode. "What were you thinking??? What will your daughter's friends think?" she sternly interrogated. The kids will not be happy over my selection and even worse, our daughter might get teased. We lived in a pretty nice community, thus everyone was worried about *keeping up with the Joneses.*

Wow! I realized there was sure a lot of pressure in buying just the *right* donuts. Now, I snapped. If I had a pressure regulator in my body, it was now on *burst open* mode and free-flowing. I had put up with a lot of flak from nearly everyone and everywhere my entire day. Now, to take more flack at home, simply because I wouldn't spend an extra $10 to be socially acceptable; was just too much to ask. The argument escalated. Other issues were brought up adding fuel to the already raging fire of animosity. My head felt hot from the drama. My ears were literally red.

Looking at the Krishna after watching this scene, I could swear it made even his all-loving heart ache a little. My heart was sure aching after watching this scene. My actions were deplorable…

Rashmi and I spent the rest of the evening in icy silence. Not wanting to fight in front of Ayaan and Diya, we attempted to engage the children in dinner conversation about their day. The children's responses to questions about their day, especially our older child, Ayaan, were usually monosyllabic responses. Answers like "Good," "Yeah," "No" or "Don't know."

After dinner, I was able to watch a few minutes of the end of the football game and the highlights on the news. I chuckled for a moment that I was watching *highlights* from the game, while I was watching *highlights of my day.* After Rashmi tucked the kids in bed, and we were in the privacy of our bedroom, we reinitiated or more accurately, reignited our argument. After a few verbal barbs *(gali's)* at each other, our tiredness and our love for each other finally quelled the flames of our animated argument. As the tension started dissipating, we apologized to each another. We truly loved each other. Yet even with all that love, arguments still happened and seemingly at a more frequent pace; as our lives became more chaotic. After we both brushed our teeth and did our routine before going to bed, the exhaustion of our day had caught up with us. We were asleep once our heads hit the pillows.

The Krishna's lips were always slightly smiling, and his composure was always highly content and peaceful. While his lips, unless he was speaking, hardly moved, I could almost swear he was smiling more after watching this scene, at least it seemed so in my imagination.

As I reflected on the reviews, my mind became quite active, as if someone gave me a shot of one of those 5-Hour energy drinks. It was a blur of cognitive function identical to a computer searching for several files at once. I wondered how I could do a better job of keeping my composure with rude drivers, demanding employees, backstabbing co-workers, strangers in the supermarket, and especially not lose it with the people I loved the most - my wife and children. I came to the realization that I lost my temper the most with one's I loved the most. I thought it was an interesting duality and wished I could come up with an answer to this dilemma. The good news, as it appeared, was that I didn't have to come up with these answers myself, and someone far wiser was going to help me get there!

Waking Up!

Ouch... I was feeling heavy, as I realized I was no longer on the beautiful *Krishna Courtyard*, and felt the heaviness of being in my physical body. I realized I woke up. It appeared I had fallen asleep in the chair in the CAT Scan waiting room. The left side of my temple hurt, as it hit the pointed top of the most uncomfortable hospital chair in history. I started thinking, "Whoever designed and worse yet purchased these chairs, did so without regard for the people sitting in them."

My inner reflection was interrupted by a tap on my shoulder and a gentle voice, "Mr. Sharma, Mr. Sharma, your son can see you now," from the nurse.

Not wanting to startle me, she said I fell asleep for about twenty minutes. She chose not to wake me, as I looked like I needed the rest. She said she had never seen someone smile and frown so many times while they were sleeping; especially for such a short interval of time.

As I was coming into my waking consciousness, I started reflecting and internally asking if I had really had a dream with a Golden Krishna. I did, however, feel very different. I was far more refreshed than any power nap I had ever taken. And, despite being in a hospital waiting room, not knowing what was going to happen to our son, I felt like I could cope with any outcome. Better than even being able to deal with the results, I felt like things were going to be okay.

Then it dawned on me. While I had learned a lot about my issues and witnessed many examples of how I needed to improve, I didn't get a chance to learn the **Three Priceless or Precious Techniques** that the Krishna alluded to. I couldn't even remember what they were called, and I wondered what I was going to do.

The nurse helped me to my feet, as I was having a little difficulty adjusting to being back in my body, and she guided me to see Ayaan. Though he should have been scared with all he had been through, Ayaan was in good spirits. I was very proud of how well he was handling the situation and himself.

The doctor came walking into the room with his head down reviewing Ayaan's files. In a very detached manner, he said that things appeared stable. Ayaan would no longer need to stay overnight and was ready to be discharged. The doctor instructed me that we should watch for symptoms like headaches, nausea, sensitivity to light and a few other things. He said that if any of these symptoms arose, to immediately bring him back in. As quickly as he spoke, he left the room, and was off to see another patient. I completed the paperwork and got Ayaan in the car. Happy to be released from the hospital, Ayaan and I drove home.

Rashmi needed to stay home during this ordeal, since she was unable to find someone to watch Ayaan. The night was supposed to be a festive one, celebrating our anniversary and celebrating Ayaan's birthday, before it went awry. Rashmi and Diya lovingly welcomed Ayaan home with hugs and kisses. We were all physically and emotionally exhausted. Leaving Ayaan's gifts unopened for another day, we all went upstairs and went to bed. We were thankful that Ayaan was home and most likely going to be OK.

The Three Priceless Techniques Dream

Exhausted from riding the emotional roller coaster of the day, I fell asleep within moments of my head hitting the pillow. It seemed like only minutes when suddenly I heard, "Rohan, the life you wished for when you were at the hospital *is possible; it does exist!"* The Krishna said, "The world of *Maya* that you are living in - is an illusion. It is an illusion of your mind..."

The Krishna was sitting on a golden chariot, patiently hovering in the air in this new dream. While his exterior was one of calmness, I could swear he inwardly was excited to share new revelations. Maybe this was just my projection, as I was so relieved and excited that he was back. His radiance showered me with a euphoria of sorts, better than anything I had ever experienced. It was clear to me that I needed to learn something more to cease the misery that I, with my own mind and emotions, was creating for myself and those around me.

While in my dream-state, I was conversing with the Krishna, doing reviews of my life and then the illusion of my life began to be clear. It was almost as if everything *was* a dream or rather, as the Krishna said, "*Maya, an illusion.*" I remembered that before we had reviewed my day, I asked the magic question, "How can I change the illusion?"

The ever-perceptive Krishna smiled and said, "Now, I will teach you **Three Priceless Techniques** that will transform your illusion and thus your suffering. Before I teach you the **First**

Priceless Technique what do you see when you look at yourself in the mirror?"

Now in the *Krishna Courtyard* appeared a full-length mirror on the wall. While I looked at the mirror, I saw a man who was looking tired, losing his hair, losing the virility of his youth, with bags under his eyes, and wrinkles on his forehead. I decided to sum up my existence by answering the Krishna with, "I see an *IT businessman.*"

Again, the Krishna didn't change his expression, but from my perspective I thought he kind of simpered. He replied, "**The First Priceless Technique** is that you need to remember *you are a Krishna* and that *you have Krishna Consciousness within you,*" he specified with such logical tone. When he spoke, his tone had this most unique quality - there was no demeaning, there were no condescension, there was just truth.

"I am a Krishna… What does this mean?" I asked.

The Krishna poetically paused for a moment and then said softly with excitement, "It implies that you have an eternal relationship with the Divine and we are always drawn either to Him directly or to His energies!

You are seeing past the dream. In other words, you are living *outside* this world of physical illusion. A Krishna no longer experiences the anguish, misery and suffering that you have experienced in your reviews. A Krishna is filled with tranquil abiding, deep peace, empathy and compassion."

He lovingly further explained, "Unfortunately Rohan, you are blocking your true Krishna Consciousness, because you are identifying yourself with *Maya* the world of illusion – the physical world that you currently live in and all the thoughts and emotions that go along with it. If you break down the word enlightenment, it literally means to *lighten the mind.* You do this by removing your heaviness caused by negative emotions and thoughts."

"yada te moha-kalilam , buddhir vyatitarisyati

tada gantasi nirvedam srotavyasya srutasya ca

In the Bhagavad Gita, chapter 2, verse 52 I have said:

When you have overcome the delusions of your understanding sprung from self –centered attachment, then you attain to a state of indifference towards all the past experiences and the others yet to be had. The deluded man, habitually, compelled by the inner voice of the sense mind, sorrows about unaccomplished experiences of the past and is greedy for the future satisfactions. The ordinary person is bound like a prisoner in a dungeon; his life experiences are narrowly confined to the dismal realm of the senses.

But the one whose intellect is illumined with spiritual knowledge no longer seeks material sense pleasures, knowing them to be harbingers of misery. The advanced yogi is so overwhelmed for having contacted the surprise of all surprises – the ever-new bliss of God – that he becomes indifferent to all thoughts of sense pleasures. He is conscious only of glorious omnipresence and its everlasting joy. The "Eternal Now" is split for man into constant states of Past, Present, and Future. In cosmic consciousness within a state of pure tranquil, these delusions of relativity disappear, and with them, the illusory dreams of past sense pleasures and unfulfilled desires, and future hope and promises. In these passages Krishna Consciousness is being discussed."

Wow! I thought this conversation was like drinking from a fire hose! For a moment, a doubt popped into my head that I wouldn't be able to understand these teachings, much less deploy them. I didn't even know what tranquil abiding meant. While being filled with deep peace sounded great, it also sounded very unrealistic. "How do I change that?" I queried.

"It's really quite simple," answered the Krishna. "Close your eyes, put your tongue on the roof of your   palate, and imagine that you are a Glowing Krishna. Keep imagining you are a Glowing Krishna of pure, bright light, then imagine that a rainbow light is emanating in concentric circles all around you. Continue to imagine these concentric circles of rainbow light growing outward to infinity and see yourself becoming an ever-expanding Glowing Krishna."

Whether *my* physical lips were actually moving or not, I couldn't tell. But in the dream, I was grinning from ear-to-ear as I started applying this **Technique**! My body felt lighter and my stress was rapidly dissipating. It was like snow being melted by the warm light and heat from the rays of the Sun. I was in awe to see how fast the **First Priceless Technique** was working. I was experiencing deeper levels of peace with each passing moment.

Physically, my shoulders felt like they sunk deep down into the bed. My breathing became deeper yet slower, and my face felt like it was glowing. "Wow*!"* I thought to myself, "This is amazing!*"*

"Rohan, the end result of this **Technique** is to bring about your true nature; you're *Krishna* Consciousness. I will now show you an advanced **Technique** that will help you even more. Please visualize me descending from the heavens, coming down in *through* the top of your head." The Krishna paused for a moment as he watched me comprehend and simulate this initial part of the **Technique**. "As you bring me down through the top of your head and into your body, you merge the me into you and you into me. From the center of your heart, you then visualize rainbow concentric circles of light spiraling outward in all ten directions. Merging with the me at the beginning is vital to the **Technique's** success, because it helps bring about the tranquil and empowering energy of the Krishna Consciousness to help you cultivate your soul merger within this consciousness. The concentric rings of light emerging from your heart help transform the environment around you."

He sagaciously paused for a moment. My mind was again like a hard drive doing a search query. I realized that by identifying myself as a businessman I was limiting myself. I was seeing only the tip of the iceberg of my true existence. To test this new **Technique**, I imagined a new mirror in the *Krishna Courtyard* and looked at myself as a businessman in the mirror. I could only hold this image for a few seconds. This image was too painful. I started feeling pressure in my head, congestion in my sinuses, and other parts of my body started feeling heavy. "Whew! I said, "Enough of that!"

I changed the image in my *Krishna Courtyard Mirror* and saw my reflection as a Krishna. "Ahhh..." resoundingly went off in my inner ears. I could feel the peace in my mind, body and soul! The Krishna was right. Being a Krishna was far better than being just a businessman. I let the mirror disappear and turned back to the Krishna.

The Krishna said it was time for learning **Priceless Technique Number Two.**

"Rohan, when you look at your world what do you see?" he asked.

I immediately thought of the review. I saw my tired body wake up in the morning, the conflicts at home, the conflicts on the freeways, the conflict at work and the conflict at the supermarket. I said, "The world is full of conflict! It is a pretty dark place."

The Glowing Krishna paused. He gently and sweetly confirmed "You are correct! The world, as you are currently seeing it, from your *Rohan perspective* is conflict, sadness, and suffering. While 'yes' there are times of happiness, these times are waning, and suffering is inevitable. As you learn to see the world through your Krishna Consciousness you'll move past the word of form and illusion that is plaguing you and others."

He drew in in a breath and his breath and presence seemed shine even more light into the dream. He said *Maya* means Him, but it also meant Sovereignty and as we started seeing past our limiting filters of our senses our eyes, feelings and etc. we become Sovereign, and are able to connect to the cosmic consciousness and become one with Spirit. To better illustrate that there is a passage in the Gita (chapter 8, verse 4) that quotes:

adhibhūtaṁ kṣharo bhāvaḥ puruṣhaśh chādhidaivatam
adhiyajño 'ham evātra dehe deha-bhṛitāṁ vara

The kaleidoscope of the universe, consisting of all manifestations of the five elements—earth, water, fire, air, space—is called *adhibhūta*. The *virāṭ puruṣh*, which is the complete cosmic personality of God encompassing the entire material creation, is called *adhidaiva* because he has sovereignty over the *devatās* (the celestial gods who administer the different departments of the universe). The Supreme Divine Personality, Shree Krishna, who dwells in the heart of all living beings as the *Paramātmā* (Supreme soul) is called *Adhiyajña*. All *yajñas* (sacrifices) are to be performed for his satisfaction. He is thus the presiding divinity over all the *yajñas* and the one who bestows rewards for all actions.

He eloquently paused to let this statement soak in. He could see that I remembered this Gita passage and he continued.

"Rohan, since you are a Hindu, you must remember that the *location* you are in, wherever you are, is a *Krishna Kingdom*. The energy that radiates from your Krishna conscience inherently can help transform the environment around you into a Krishna Kingdom," he clarified. **"Priceless Technique Number Two** is seeing the environment around you and the world in general as a Krishna Kingdom. You see past the illusion and see the environment as pure radiant light! In the same way that you saw yourself as a Krishna, which was a limited view of yourself, your limited perception is seeing only the darkness in the world. Yes, there is darkness in the world, but you can help transform it." he concluded.

"In the Gita, Chapter 6, verse 30 it is said, 'He who perceives Me everywhere and beholds everything in Me never loses sight of Me, nor do I ever lose sight of him'. To lose me means to let the mind wander away from my presence, and to be with me means to unite the mind with him. The easy way to unite the mind with me is to learn to see everything in its connection with me.

'Therefore, nothing can exist without me and Krishna consciousness is the development of love of Krishna. This verse also points out that the illumined being does not lose the individuality of his soul; instead he finds his being extended into the Being of the Spirit. A Krishna Kingdom is the derivative of such intimate relationship of Krishna and his devotees and the collective expansion of love that exists in your midst.' Krishna Kingdom is a little catchier, is it not?" he said to me with a wink.

I was so startled by his eloquent grace and now his display of humor. I thought to my "Wow, I'm speaking with the Krishna in a dream and he is cracking a joke!" We were so serious, and I was learning these deep teachings and maybe he thought I needed a little humor to lighten them mood.

Just learning that I was a Krishna was a big mental upgrade. If I was a computer I felt like jumped up several levels in my operating system software. It was like I went from DOS to Windows 10. The idea that my being had an effect on my locale was the equivalent of moving from a using a floppy disc to a Two Terabyte hard drive.

Inquisitively, I closed my eyes and imagined the world around me transforming into a Krishna Kingdom. I visualized the Kingdom of Krishna and its ebullient light illumining my surroundings. Feeling an even greater level of peace, it now donned on me that peace had levels… My inner chatter slowed. It almost stopped, or rather just silenced.

My inner dialogue was now gone. Well almost gone, as my inner dialogue chose to fight back. It attempted to fill my head once again with chatter. In an attempt to preserve itself, the dialogue tried to start up again by talking about the lack of talking. It was almost humorous.

Again, I empowered my inner dialogue to subside with greater ease than before. In its place, I experienced stillness and a level of love that I had never encountered before. It was deeper than the love I felt when I held my newborn child for the very first time. The sweetness was sublime. I was in a total state of bliss!

With these profound changes, I was also noticing in my mind and emotions, that there was a corresponding effect on my physical body. As my mind became clearer in thought and quicker in response, my physical eyes felt brighter. The congestion that was normally present in my sinus passages started clearing up, and the underlying tension in my neck and shoulders started loosening. As my newly found bliss started increasing, my breathing repetition slowed, and the tension in my chest released. It seemed there was a relationship between this release of tension and the decreasing of my heartbeat. This was a welcome relief for my hypertension, which I suffered from for many years. I could feel my blood pressure slow as my breathing pattern eased.

"Everything in this physical world is an illusion. In ancient Sanskrit they called it Maya and is based on your perception. Photons, for example, are totally invisible until they strike your retina. Sugar is tasteless until it strikes your tongue. A rose has no fragrance until your nose inhales the pleasant aroma. The sound of a tree falling doesn't exist until your eardrums make it so. These qualities (technically known as qualia) are produced by the mechanism of perception." To further the point, he added, "Most people would think the color of the Sun is orange or yellow. However, the filter of the earth's energy field and your eyes give it the hue of these colors. When seen from space it is actually blinding white light!" With the brilliance of a Krishna, he eloquently discoursed.

I could mentally see a foreshadowing of a future event; my doctor explaining that I would no longer need my high blood pressure medication. This process was like being in an imaginary spa that worked out the tightness in my body as the serenity of this healing space melted my tension away.

I shared with the Krishna that the people in my imaginary Krishna Kingdom were glowing and smiling. I could feel an electrical buzz in the air that was filled with waves of energy. My new level of consciousness seemed to enable me to feel deeper levels of peace, stillness and love. The feelings were similar to those I felt radiating from the Krishna, but to a lesser degree.

"Very good, Rohan, you are learning quickly," the Krishna confidently praised.

"As you've experienced your Krishna Consciousness, your true nature Rohan, it is very easy to imagine that you are a Krishna. It is very easy to imagine that all that is around you is a Krishna Kingdom, or, in reality the Kingdom of God. Over time, with practice, you will not have to work at this process. It will be easier, and you will be transformed into this natural state," he articulated.

"With practice, O Parth, when you constantly engage the mind in remembering me, the Supreme Divine Personality, without deviating, you will certainly attain me'. **Gita 8: 8** quotes this.

It is important to remember that what we think with our mind fashions our future, not the actions we perform with our body. It is the mind that is to be engaged in devotion, and it is the mind that is to be surrendered to God. And when the absorption of the consciousness in God is complete, one will receive the divine grace. By God's grace, one will attain liberation from material bondage, and will receive the unlimited divine bliss, divine knowledge, and divine love of God. Such a soul will become God-realized in this body itself and will go to the abode of God. In this passage it means you Rohan, must create this abode of God on earth.

You are a co-creator in this process. You need to do this for yourself, to help you with our own suffering and to transform for the darkness, war, and the lower natures of man. If they say to you: 'It is in the sea,' then the fishes will precede you. Rather, the kingdom is inside of you and outside of you. When you come to know yourselves, then you will be known, and you will realize that you are the children of the living God. But if you do not come to know yourselves, then you exist in poverty, and you are poverty," he profoundly stated.

He wisely paused to allow me to grasp these verses and continued with,

"teshām evānukampārtham aham ajñāna-jaṁ tamaḥ
nāśhayāmyātma-bhāva-stho jñāna-dīpena bhāsvatā

From sheer compassion, I, the Divine Indweller, set alight in them the radiant lamp of wisdom which banishes the darkness that is born of ignorance". To put it simply, by his grace, God bestows his divine senses, divine mind, and divine intellect to the soul. Equipped with these divine instruments, the soul is able to see God, hear God, know God, and be united with God. Rohan, once you use this God given intelligence to ask the right questions, follow the right actions and demand enlightenment, His Grace lights up the inner wisdom-lamp in you, dispelling the dark shadows of ignorance. You now become the light of the world and let your inner light shine and create this Krishna Kingdom on earth!

"One of my favorite versus, he said, is also from the **Gita 11:4**

O Lord of all mystic powers, if you think I am strong enough to behold it, then kindly reveal that imperishable cosmic form to me, Arjuna said: "O Yogeshwar, I have expressed my wish. If you consider me worthy of it, then by your grace, please reveal your cosmic form to me, and show me your *Yog-aishwarya* (mystic opulence)."

It is said that one can neither see, hear, understand nor perceive the Supreme Lord, Krishna, by the material senses. If the infinite reveals Himself, then it is possible to understand the nature of the infinite by the grace of the infinite. The word *Yogeshwar* is also very significant here because the Lord has inconceivable power. If He likes, He can reveal Himself by His grace, although He is unlimited, and His kingdom is spread out upon the earth and people do not see it.

"Just to recap Rohan, your job is to seek the Krishna Kingdom consciously, which is the higher form of *Maya,* and by helping to build the Krishna Kingdom on earth, you become Sovereign. *"But you cannot see Me with your present eyes. Therefore, I give to you divine eyes by which you can behold My mystic opulence"*
"To see the universal form of Krisna, Arjuna is told not to change his mind but his vision. The Lord gives him the particular vision required to see that universal form because Arjuna is the beginning of the paramapara system. Those who need to find this universal presence of Krishna need to follow Arjuna's steps and build on his legacy to find the supreme destination of this Krishna Kingdom, He shared.

I was overjoyed at hearing about these scriptures and now understanding them at an entirely new level.

Similar to how I tested the concepts learned with **Priceless Techniques Number One**, I imagined looking at the world from my normal *Rohan perspective*. Talk about a crash landing... I literally felt like I was dropped from the heavens when I looked at the world through these *Maya goggles*. The world looked even darker than before, the people that I worked with looked a little *ghoulish*.

I quickly reverted my vision back to my *Krishna Vision (Dhrishti)*. Instead of seeing just the conflicts and alike, I now saw the people from as Souls. I got a glimpse on how these conflicts darkened their Souls with hideous energies around them. It was a little scary, but I know understood why people were literally chained to suffering without this *Krishna Vision (Dhrishti)*

The Krishna observed that I was getting a little scared at this new realization. Seeing the true nature of others was a little shocking, but I think he knew that I could handle it. It was probably best that I realized that I was on this path of being tethered to *Samsara and* seeing this new reality would provide extra motivation to get out of it!

The Krishna poetically paused and asked, "Are you ready for **Priceless Technique Number Three?**"

I got the feeling by the way he said it that this **Technique** was going to be harder. The first two were pretty easy, so there must be some sort of catch with the third. Maybe I had to put myself into some yogic pretzel for 24 hours, wonder in the dessert for 40 days, fly off to the Himalayas, give away all my worldly possessions or walk around in a G-string and grow a beard. These were the visuals that popped into my head. I wondered what it could be, and with inner exuberance and a slight apprehension, I answered, "Yes!"

"As I said," the Krishna continued, "The first two **Techniques** are very easy to apply. The **Third** is also easy; however, most people will find it difficult to apply at first. With practice, this technique will be the most rewarding for you, and it will also help others the most as well!"

"Rohan imagine seeing someone that you love," he said. I immediately imagined my daughter, Ayaan. "She is so sweet and adorable," I thought to myself. The Krishna could see my smiling. "Rohan," he countered "Imagine someone you don't like." I imagined one of my co-workers and in mind's eye. She looked like a witch. In fact, I imagined hearing her fake laugh, sounded like a witch's, chilling laugh."

I started hearing her say "My pretty..." and the Krishna wisely interrupted with "What is the difference in how you *see* these people?"

"I had never really thought it. The way I saw others just popped into my head, it just seemed normal to judge others. I thought for a moment and replied, "When I see Ayaan I'm focused on her good qualities and my co-worker's negative qualities stick out like a sore thumb." I replied.

The Krishna started a new declaration, "As you learned in the **First Two Priceless Techniques** the world you are living in is an illusion, like a dream, a world of your ordinary perceptions. The physical world is an illusion, and the real world is the Kingdom of God, where everything is light. The Essenes knew that everything is light. It is interesting that science is still trying to teach that there is a speed of light, when everything is light. Most people when they read the Gita miss the clue in **Chapter 4:1** "The Blessed Lord said: I instructed this imperishable science of yoga to the sun-god, Vivasvan, and Vivasvan instructed it to Manu, the father of mankind, and Manu in turn instructed it to Iksvaku"

Human life is meant for cultivation of spiritual knowledge, in eternal relationship with the Supreme Personality of Godhead, and the executive heads of all states and all planets are obliged to impart this lesson to the citizens by education, culture and devotion. The sun is the king of the planets, and the sun-god (at present of the name Vivasvan) rules the sun planet, which is controlling all other planets by supplying heat and light and is rotating under the order of Krishna.

In science light is said to travel at approximately 186,000 miles per second. The symbolism here is the instruction to the sun to transmit the light in Divine order. You now have a greater understanding of that reality, from when you turned into a Krishna and saw the world as a Krishna Kingdom and see everything as light!"

"When you were annoyed with drivers on the freeway, irritated with your boss, maddened by your co-workers, aggravated with people in the grocery store, and upset with your children and your wife; all of these thoughts and emotions were emanating from your *non-Krishna Consciousness nature.* You are seeing darkness... To make matters worse, the negative perceptions you held towards these people projected negative energies at them. These negative energies affected *their internal organs, their energy Kingdom* and further diminished *their Krishna conscience within.* Along with this damage to them, there was also a rebound effect as it damaged you as well."

"So," maintained the Krishna, "Since you are a Krishna, having *Krishna Consciousness,* you would never harm anyone or anything. By applying this principle, you certainly wouldn't hurt anyone physically, nor would you hurt anyone with your mind (your thoughts) or your speech."

He paused for a moment to let this sink in. The depth of his words touched my heart and touched the depths of my soul. The Krishna was right. I had never thought about harming others with thought.

"Each person whether you chose to like them, or not is just like you. They are just people on their way to reaching their Krishna Nature. Some are farther down the path than others. Many have just started. This is **Priceless Technique Number Three,** you must remember that others are Krishnas too, and to see them as Krishnas!" he finished.

For the first time in my dreams with the Krishna, I was a little disenchanted. I felt some trepidation as to whether I could actually apply this last precious pearl of wisdom that the Krishna had so freely given me. Just like when I was fantasizing in line at the supermarket of having a life that movie stars led, my fantasy easily slipped away when a cart hit me in the back. I could feel my consciousness and energy contracting with the return of my inner dialogue.

"

"suhrn-mitrary-udasina-madhyastha-dvesya-bandhusu
sadhusv api ca papesu ; sama-buddhir visisyate"

He is a supreme yogi who regards with equal mindedness all men – patrons, friends, enemies, strangers, mediators, hateful beings, relatives, the virtuous and the ungodly. The yogi is one who similarly regards all human beings - friends and enemies, saints and sinners alike – as dream image made of the one consciousness of God. The exalted yogi, however does not treat gold and earth, saint and sinner, with impartial indifference!

The entire universe, with all its living and non-living beings is the manifestation of the Supreme Being, who dwells within It." *purusha evedam sarvam* (Purush Sūktam) [v3] "God is everywhere in this world, and everything is his energy." Hence, the highest yogi sees everyone as the manifestation of God and attunes to Divine forgiveness.

From the now jaded perspective, I believe the Krishna tried to give me reassurance by sharing more scriptures to inspire me. I just realized the word "inspire" means "in spirit." I know realized that all beings were Children of God and embodies in the Divine

Light of the Cosmic Consciousness! WOW!!! My mind was blown. I could have sworn the Krishna gave me an even bigger smile, as he saw consciousness was expanding and become more Krishna-like. I could have sworn he said, "There will be more on this later!"

With profound wisdom and compassion, the Krishna suggested that I simply give it a try. He said, "Imagine yourself at the office in a sales meeting, and see your boss complimenting you for exceeding your sales quota, then taking it away by saying you needed to do more in the next quarter."

The Krishna's smile and the simplicity of his words put me at ease. His radiance was something to behold. I reflected that, under these circumstances, my co-workers would have feelings of jealousy. They would only hear the compliment part, and conveniently ignore the next quarter part of the communication. Also, while they might not outwardly show it, they would unconsciously be glaring at me with the energy of envy. Now I was able to feel this *envy energy* even in the dream. The Krishna stated that the world of energy was more *real* than the physical realm. Recalling these words, it became clear I was full of understanding.

I loved being on the *Krishna Courtyard* as it brought out my *Krishna Intelligence,* too. I was able to easily put concepts together. I reflected on expressions that we used daily and how the colors used in these idioms reflected energy. "Green with envy," meant jealousy. "Feeling blue today," denoted sadness. "A yellow-belly," reflected someone who was afraid. "My ears are burning (red)..." demonstrated how dirty, red emotional energy was being directed at others. "Whoa! I loved these realizations!" I concluded.

It now donned on me that as a Krishna, I would also have access to omniscience, as well. I could swear the Krishna did one of those *smiles at yet another realization* and said, "Let's continue..."

The Krishna told me to once again imagine myself becoming as a Krishna of pure golden light with rainbow light emanating, and then to see the boardroom and the building as a Krishna Kingdom. The Krishna stated to re-imagine my boss and co-workers turning into Krishnas of pure golden light by applying **Priceless Technique Number Three.** With apprehension, I followed the steps, and much to my amazement; I felt an incredible sense of lightness. I was now feeling bliss taking me even higher than I had felt earlier in the dream. "Wow, the Krishna was right!" I gleefully said in my head. "This **Priceless Technique** was the crown jewel of the **Three!!!**

He further added, that if at any time I was in a rush, or having challenges imagining gold and rainbow light, that I could substitute pure light. And, see everything as pure light!

I couldn't remember if what a Gita quote or not, but I remembered always hearing "Find God in all things, or in other words 'Find God in others' was meant something entirely new to me.

In this moment of reflection, I realized a profound similarity. The similarity of being and seeing people as pure golden light. I remembered that the word *enlightenment* meant making the mind light, and not entangled with gray, dirty, heavier energy. "Light felt good," I thought.

To recap Rohan, when you see others through the filter of your heart and your Krishna Consciousness you are fulfilling the mission stated in **Gita 8:4** "Physical nature is known to be endlessly mutable. The universe is the cosmic form of the Supreme Lord, and I am that Lord represented as the Supersoul, dwelling in the heart of every embodied being".

My lips seemingly moved on their own accord as I started smiling. I never realized until now just how much stress I had previously carried in my facial muscles, let alone the rest of my body. It seemed as I was becoming *lighter,* it was easier to want to stay in this state.

"How many people know about these **Three Priceless Techniques?**" I asked.

"Not enough," wittily replied the Krishna.

Who would have thought that the Krishna, along with his omniscience, also possessed humor, timing and wit? I thought it might have been my imagination, but I could also feel a sense of sadness emanating from the Krishna. I realized it wasn't sadness, but rather compassion. I could feel him wanting others to know of these **Techniques**. I also saw in his body language, that he wanted people to stop ignorantly hurting each other with their words, thoughts and interactions. This realization gave me a boost of energy - a confidence and a purpose. I felt like I was part of something bigger than myself.

"Well," I said, "how many people would be enough?"

"Great question!" the Krishna fired back. "There are approximately seven billion people on the physical world on earth. If seven million or more would apply the **Three Priceless Techniques**, it would create a wave of energy, literally a positive tsunami of energy. If done simultaneously and consistently, it could transform the physical world into a Krishna Kingdom... *forever.*"

The Krishna further explained when a person becomes a Krishna, their energy Kingdom expands more than ten times. As they create a Krishna Kingdom, the frequency of that location is also purified and multiplied by yet another ten plus times. And, as other people do it together at the same location, the energy is multiplied by still another ten-fold. He alluded to speaking more about the group application of these **Priceless Techniques** at another time and how it dramatically multiplied everything.

"So you see Rohan, the Earth needs at least seven million people doing these **Techniques** simultaneously," the Krishna concluded.

I mentally did the math. 7,000,000 people multiplying their energy 10 times, the energy of the location 10 times and simultaneously multiplying the energy of others by 10; that might just equal seven hundred million people, or roughly $1/10^{th}$ of 1% of the population. The wave of Krishna Kingdoms from this number of people could be enough to help all seven billion people. The Krishna seemed to be smiling even more, so I was on to something. I thought it was pretty cool I could do math in a dream!

A New Day

Boom! I landed in my body... Crash landing into the physical world felt very heavy. The alarm was screeching... While it was still an annoying sound, in my head, I transformed the claxon sound to be playing U2's *A Beautiful Day.* The Krishna dream was gone, however, the remnants of what he taught me remained. It was now time for the reality and heaviness of the physical world. As the weight of my hand hit the alarm clock, it seemed lighter than usual.

I collected myself as I showered. My negative internal dialogue started... I now dubbed it o*ld Rohan Talk* and it tried to deny the dream's existence. My newfound countenance quickly shrugged it off. It now also seemed as if the world of dreams and the *real* world were merging... With the highest mental and emotional clarity that I had ever experienced, I recounted the **Three Priceless Techniques,** *"Become a Krishna, check! Transform the surrounding area into a Krishna Kingdom (the Kingdom of God or, pure light), check! And, most importantly, visualize everyone in that Krishna Kingdom as a Krishna of pure golden rainbow light emanating around them, check!"*

In the shower, I imagined myself as a Krishna. I felt the anticipated stress of the day begin to melt away, just like it had happened in the dream. I could feel my sinuses clearing, my shoulders relaxing, and my blood pressure dropping. These physical responses were confirmation that the **Technique** was working.

I then imagined the house, in all its hustle and bustle, as a Krishna Kingdom and my lovely wife and children as Krishnas. I chuckled as I saw Rashmi and the kids as Krishnas. It was very easy to do, since I loved them so much.

I saw my son Ayaan smiling, recalling his state of mind just a few nights before. I realized the experience of being in the hospital was over, and it now felt more like a bad dream. It was amazing knowing that while the concussion experience did occur, my emotions, attachments and suffering were transformed after the review. For lack of a better explanation, the experience was like a *bad dream* and now only a distant, fleeting memory.

As we each prepared for the day and ate breakfast, there seemed to be a rhythm to the house. The energy of the house seemed to slow down quite a bit – as if the house was relaxed, too. Each task was accomplished with greater ease and efficiency than usual. It seemed as if Rashmi, Ayaan and Diya each had a slight smile on each of their faces. I, in particular, had a smile on my face watching this new, surreal *real* world happen before my eyes.

Hugging Rashmi while leaving out the front door was magical! When our bodies met, it felt like our energy Kingdoms merged, as if to create an electrical spark! The positive energy of the house seemed to also affect our physical chemistry. I didn't want to leave her embrace and looked forward to more of this sensation when I got home.

As I drove down the familiar 405 highway, I visualized the bumper-to-bumper traffic as a Krishna Kingdom of multi-colored, metallic lotus flowers each carrying Krishnas. I really liked this creative visualization and thought the Krishna would be proud of my improvisation. Within a few minutes of driving two drivers cut me off. After two of these *asphalt battles*, I would normally have been yelling at them, or worse. Instead, I mentally blessed them with greater awareness and consideration towards their fellow drivers. Each time I did this, I noticed my demeanor serene. As if by magic, the cutting off stopped... Normally each negative event would worsen my mood, escalate my negative emotions and elevate my blood pressure. Now, each negative experience was transformed into a positive one. These **Techniques** were truly transformative, as each negative interaction made me feel even better! The rest of the drive flowed with ease, and I soon arrived in the office parking lot. Instead of feeling drained, I felt invigorated!

Samantha, the receptionist, was engaged in multiple conversations and looked stressed. I immediately saw the office as a Krishna Kingdom, and saw her transforming into a Krishna of luminous, golden light. I imagined the rainbow light that she was radiating going through the phone. As I walked past her, I thought I could feel her rainbow Kingdom of energy changing. If I wasn't mistaken, it appeared to grow larger and gently merge through mine. Our collective energies were merging, and we were transforming the environment together. This interaction planted seeds within my consciousness for later exploration.

Grasping the handle of my office door, I heard her tone change and could hear that she was surely smiling as she warmly greeted new callers and effortlessly helped re-connect those on hold. "So far so good," I thought. "This was easy!"

The Company Meeting

Placing my briefcase on the desk, I pulled out my iPad and clicked on the calendar app. At the top of the daily calendar view *8 AM, Product Steering Committee Meeting* in Conference Room A.

While peering out the office window to take in the spectacular site below, I checked my watch. "It was 7:53 AM, just enough time to visit the men's room and walk upstairs to the meeting," I planned.

As I walked into the conference room, my *Krishna Suit* was starting to fray and come apart at the seams. My o*ld Rohan Chatter* reared its ugly head. It tried to pull my mood down by suggesting how long and boring this meeting would be. I imagined the voice moving farther and farther away from me, and it disappeared. I believe I read somewhere that the Buddhist version of Angels were called *Dakinis.* As the negative talk was moving further away in my consciousness, it felt like these *Dakinis* were like little seamstresses repairing my *Krishna Suit.*

By 8:20 the usual routine had occurred; consisting of a review of the prior week, projections for this week, and I was both praised and pressured by my boss. The praise lacked sincerity-feeling more like lip service. The pressure was always there. My weekly goals were the highest of the team, as there were always high-expectations of my results.

My boss Raghu was more concerned about his own success, though. While some managers like to empower leaders, his style was to create followers. I watched many times how, instead of empowering people and supporting them; he just took their territories away and made excuses to justify it.

The more I succeeded, the more he wanted to remind me who was the boss. However, when I underperformed, the blame fell on me... He was always quick to remind us that his boss, Mr. Stuebe chose him for the job to manage us.

The toughest part of these meetings wasn't how Jackson made me feel, but the palpable envy from my co-workers and from Julie Perez, in particular. As much as I tried to ignore her, the fact was that Julie was a fiery and power-hungry salesperson. She wanted to take my position within the company. In fact, she wanted it so badly she maximized every opportunity to create a division between Jackson and me. She had a master plan... She had her sights on Jackson's boss, the CEO and President, Charles Stuebe and to be his *Hand of King.* Julie had even resorted to power plays and innuendos, which had really damaged my reputation in the company for the past eighteen months.

Sitting in the conference room, I thought to myself, "Seeing my family as Krishnas and seeing another driver's as Krishnas, was easy. But how could I possibly see Julie as a Krishna? It would have been easier to view her as a devil than a Krishna..."

The meeting dragged on, as these meetings tended to do, with each person adding lengthy and poorly communicated mini-filibusters. In spite of the boredom I was experiencing, I was having no problem seeing myself as a Krishna. As I mentally recalled past meetings with Jackson and Julie, my *Krishna Suit* started fading. With this inner struggle, I had to work harder to re-amplify my Krishna splendor. The visual of the conference room as a Krishna Kingdom, and my co-workers as Krishnas emanating golden and rainbow light was a struggle to hold in my mind. These steps were being pretty well executed until jealousy reared its ugly head. Julie was torching me with her *mental flamethrower.* My emotional and mental state dropped instantly... My finely tailored *Krishna Suit* was now developing holes and looked like it was purchased at the Goodwill.

I tried to laugh it off by imagining the fire was only singeing my suit, and not burning it; but, to no avail..

I could no longer even feel the smooth buzz of the imagined Krishna Kingdom, as the light diminished. I could now feel prickly, hot energy coming at me, slung effusively and carelessly by Julie.

I started feeling like the *old Rohan*, my old self; pre-anything Krishna related Rohan... Instead of feeling empowered and *Krishna-like,* I felt very disappointed with myself. I started even feeling less than the *old Rohan,* because I thought I should have been better at applying the **Techniques.** I had moved so far forward, at least so I thought. Now, I had regressed backwards even further... My sinuses were acting up. I again had tension in my head, neck and back. I also felt like I needed to take my hypertension medication. I felt like a failure.

I came to the conclusion that if I was observant, my body would tell me what I needed to work on. I pondered, "Awareness is a powerful thing!"

Before the dream, I was more somber than depressed. Having felt bliss and peace, I now knew what being depressed felt like, and I now felt it. Now, more than anything I wanted inner peace! This vacillation of my emotions, and thus suffering, was maddening.

My breathing raced uncontrollably; my thoughts soared around like vultures in my headspace. I replayed the Krishna dream over and over again in my head, but I wasn't able to come up with a solution as to how to handle this particular situation.

The Three Priceless Techniques were truly priceless, and now appeared as if they were no longer afforded to me. My inner dialogue went to a negative place. My *old Rohan Talk* was cutting my *Krishna Suit* to shreds. I was now doubting that I could have success applying the **Techniques**. "Sure, these **Techniques** worked in dreams, but this was real life after all," I ruminated.

After the meeting, I went back to my office and closed the door. I recomposed myself by doing the visualizations. I sought to bring myself out of this *old Rohan*-style funk, by applying the **Three Priceless Techniques**. After a few minutes, I still wasn't feeling 100% *Krishna-like*, but concluded I was maybe at 72%. From the depths of disappointment, to back being somewhat *Krihna-like*, this achievement was still pretty remarkable. I reflected on the gamut of emotions that I was experiencing on a daily basis. I resolved that I wanted to maintain this *tranquil abiding* state of being that the Krishna wisely referenced. It was at this moment, I made the mental resolution to end this emotional vacillation!

I had to drop off some forecasts to Cheryl, Jackson's secretary. She always treated me dispassionately. She was young, lacked education, and had no real business experience prior to Jackson hiring her. Jackson valued her devotion and loyalty to him and him alone. "Maybe it was because he hired Cheryl without any experience that she reciprocated this loyalty?" I mused. She usually spoke with employees on Jackson's behalf, in a demeaning manner, which typically left them with a bad taste in their mouth. We weren't very motivated by Jackson as a whole, or as she reminded us to call him, "Mr. Jones."

Little did Jackson realize that his choice in an assistant cost him production, as her coldness demotivated us even more. This whole interaction dropped me further down on the *Krishna scale to* maybe 34% *Krishna-like.*

The Christ said it would take work, diligence and time. I hoped it wouldn't take too long for me to act *Krishna-like* on a regular basis. My *Krishna Suit* was regaining form and replaced my inner dialogue with thinking, "Thirty-four percent Krishna-like was certainly better than 100% *old Rohan-like.*" The awareness of my self-talk was really coming to the forefront of my consciousness. And, more importantly, I was able to distinguish which voice was winning; *old Rohan* or *Krishna-like Rohan.*

The drive home was better. This transition from work to my home was exceeding my hopes. I again visualized the cars as metallic lotus flowers floating over the pavement and carrying their Krishna safely home. This visualization always made me chuckle, and I hoped the Krishna would be proud of my improvisation of **Techniques Two and Three.** I was much more relaxed, and I even smiled a few times; even when a few cars cut me off. I made it home about seven minutes quicker than normal.

The interactions at home were also better. In fact, they were incredible! The connectedness amongst my family was at an all-time high! I felt like I was not only becoming more sensitive to my own energy Kingdom, but to the energy Kingdom of those around me. It felt as if our collective energy Kingdoms melted into one. Rashmi, Ayaan, Diya, I seemed to merge our gold and rainbow energy Kingdoms into one large, powerful Kingdom. The Kingdom briefly mentioned that he'd speak with me again about the power of groups, and I was now looking forward to that conversation.

The ability to sense this energetic connection with others was very precious. I mentally flashed back to my family's chaotic interaction from yesterday and was happy that these same three people were glowing so brightly. My positive feelings for them were also magnified. It was pretty cool making our home into a Krishna Kingdom with four powerful Krishna's radiating rainbow lights concentrically to infinity!

Once my body was lying in bed and my head hit the pillow, I reviewed my day and was quite pleased with the positive development. I was happy with myself that I had overcome this bump in the road. Everything was just as the Krishna had explained, mostly ups with some downs. Overall, I was prevailing in elevating my consciousness, and willingly sharing the *Krishna energies* with those around me. Yes, there were some downs to overcome, but I was confident that I would prevail. I had never had so much optimism in my life. I felt this to be my new reality. With an even lighter heart and state of being, I drifted off into a deep slumber.

As I slept, my consciousness was taken to a Krishna Kingdom. Back on the *Krishna Kingdom* the Krishna complimented me on a job well done. This time I was even more aware of the Krishna's presence, and seemed to be even more receptive to his teachings. "More alert, if that was possible in this dream?" I laughed inwardly. I somewhat reluctantly and ashamedly asked the Krishna, "How could I do better with **Priceless Technique Number Three,** particularly with someone whom I was not altogether very fond of, like Julie?"

I laughed at the words coming out of my mouth in this dream "not altogether fond of..." The Krishna knew I would have normally said, "a witch like Julie." While he again didn't change his demeanor, nor his facial expression, I could swear my new verbiage made him chuckle, too.

The Krishna, with a firm but compassionate tone, said, "Rohan, being on an emotional roller coaster is *un-Krishna like.* It is a human tendency that you must endeavor to transcend. Highs and lows, emotionally and mentally, are only based on perceptions of the physical world - a transitory world," he said.

"Remember Rohan," the Krishna continued, "The 'tranquil abiding' part of the teachings? You need to maintain a sense of peace and tranquility always, no matter what is happening."

This time, I gratefully grasped this concept on a much deeper level.

"Precious Rohan let me give you a few more methods to accomplish **Priceless Technique Number Three.** These will make it easier for you to deal with people in your life such as Julie" he proclaimed.

"The normal method is to visualize the person in the form of a Krishna, as you have done." He further clarified by saying, "Except this time, do not see them as a person in their physical body, but rather dissolve their form into formless white light, like a ball of energy with consciousness. This will help you to detach from your perception of their human qualities. Remember how you felt tonight when you and your family melted together into one energy Kingdom?" he queried.

He paused for a moment seeing whether I grasped this concept. Seeing that I had, he proceeded. "This **Technique** will be easier to use on people like Julie because you can depersonalize your *Samsaric*, physical world perceptions of people and realize that we are all one. Physically, yes, we are separate, but spiritually were are all one." He eloquently proclaimed.

His profoundness comforted me.

"Additionally, let me give you another method that will help you get to **Priceless Technique Three** with greater ease," the Krishna went on. "To help you develop more compassion for others, you can visualize any person as your own mother," the Krishna explained.

"My mother???" I interrupted.

I just realized that in this dream state with the Krishna, thinking thoughts and speaking were the same thing. In previous dreams, we sometimes communicated without our lips moving. I made a mental note to discuss this communication concept more with the Krishna at a later juncture.

"Yes, your mother!" replied the Krishna. The Krishna further answered, reading my mind. "Your mother experienced great pain in delivering you. She fed you. She changed your diapers and kept you safe. She also made many sacrifices for your betterment. A mother loves her child more than she loves herself. If you visualize every person as your mother and treat them with the same level of love and respect; in time it will help you overcome your previous negative tendencies and projections towards that person. Besides Rohan," the Krishna added with a twinkle in his eye, "She just might have been your mother in a previous life."

After his poetic pause, he went on to say, "When you've interacted in the past with Jackson's assistant Cheryl, you were concentrating on the feeling of her being cold to you.

Concentrating on this coldness diminishes the loving energy in your heart and in her heart. While, yes, it would be most ideal if Julie was easier to work with, but this is not to be expected by everyone. There are four main energetic compositions that each person has inherently created, and hers is more inward. We will cover these four compositions more in the future."

With regards to Julie, "You are correct in that she has negative intent towards you, and we'll work on that later; however, you have more work to do on yourself. Meanwhile, she is still young, and you need to tap into the creative powers of your Krishna Nature, and see her growing into a more effervescent being," explained the Krishna.

I pondered, "Wow, I'm learning a lot here, but there is still more to go!"

"I will give you yet another method, Rohan, because in time you will be sharing these **Three Priceless Techniques** with others, and you will need different strategies for different people. For people with *pride* as their stumbling block, they can rapidly diminish this pride by visualizing others as a Krishna and prostrating at their feet.

"Prostrate?" blurted out of my mouth, while I was thinking, *you have got to be kidding me...* I exclaimed "How can you prostrate in front of someone you don't like or respect?"

The Krishna responded patiently, "Would you prefer working off the karma of the relationship this way - by mentally doing prostrations and overcoming your own pride? Or, would you rather maybe, lose your prostate? I thought I heard the Krishna making a dirty joke to emphasize the correlation. Or, maybe that was just my dirty imagination. I was beginning to understand the Krishna on a higher level. I felt as if some of my bad habits, or in this case, my bad humor, was coming up and being cleared.

The Krishna paused allowing me this time to reflect. When he continued he said, "When pride is a major stumbling block, life will knock you to your knees.... Pride will cause you to have relationship challenges, financial challenges, or health challenges. Pride will drop you to your knees, it is up to you how you get there... You can do physical prostrations, mental prostrations to negate this pride, or *real-life* painful scenarios that will drive you to the floor. The choice is up to you, Rohan."

It was the first time the Krishna had been so lovingly direct with me. I reflected that, when presented this way, the Krishna's teaching along with his demeanor, had a fatherly aspect to it. It moved me. It nudged me out of my own ego, and into the realization that this **Technique** might work. And...I really needed to make it work. I realized that I still had some pride to work on. Imagining myself prostrating to a person full of pride would be challenging to my ego at first, but I believed that it would be very, very effective.

I judged Jackson as having a lot of pride, so I took control of the dream. The *Krishna Courtyard* was like a laboratory for testing theories. I came to realize it was there for my sole betterment. I chuckled, "The word *sole in sole betterment* was probably a typo, as it was surely *soul betterment.*" "I loved the realizations I made from my time with the Krishna," I further thought.

I continued with testing the concept of prostrations. "Since, we are all one," I thought "that if Jackson has pride than I must to some degree have pride, too!" I could feel my *Krishna Suit* looking particularly regal. I started at first with a bow, like is commonly practiced in Japan. I felt the area around my heart and the top of my head expand. "So far so good," I mentally said.

Maybe, it was my *pride,* but I felt like I had to transform Jackson into a bigger Krishna to prostrate in his general direction. My *Krishna Suit* now felt like it needed dry cleaning, as I was clearly judging Jackson. In my mind, I completely transformed Jackson into huge, golden Krishna. I initiated the prostrating at Jackson's now Krishna feet. After about the third, mental prostration, I felt the dry-cleaning soap washing Krishna Suit and I started to feel like I was an even larger golden Krishna. "Hmm…" I considered, "Maybe, whatever I see myself prostrating towards, I become?"

I perceived Jackson's biggest issue as pride. I pondered about Julie for a moment. I viewed her as far eviller. At this moment, I didn't honestly feel ready to prostrate towards her. The Krishna watched me and said, "Rohan, a diamond has many facets. Truth has many levels." It is good that you help her reach her potential as a Krishna. As you develop further we'll work on **Techniques** for someone who has evil intent and how to minimize it."

He continued, "Lastly, Rohan there is a simple **Technique** that can be done anywhere at any time. It is particularly great in a business situation, where you do not have a lot of time, and you find yourself losing your cool. You can mentally visualize the other person as a Krishna and say *Namaste*. *Namaste* simply means, the Krishna within me salutes the Krishna within you. This method will help melt away the mental, emotional and karmic obscurations that you have for the other person, and that they have for you. The more challenged the relationship is, the more you need to do the *Namaste* **Technique**. Your connections with others travel through different levels, but let's save that for another time."

The Next Sales Meeting

At the next weekly sales meeting, I put the **Techniques** to the test. I felt like I was at the spiritual gym, and this time I was going to cover the heavy weights section. Heavy weights have greater resistance, and thus build bigger muscles, or in this case, more developed spiritual muscles.

Mentally, I remade myself into a Krishna seeing the room as a Krishna Kingdom. I visualized everyone in the room as a Krishna emitting gold and rainbow light, especially Julie. I made a major transformation in the way I saw her. I was now grateful for her. Rather than seeing her as an impediment or opponent, I now saw her as an instrument to my personal growth - as a teacher. I concentrated on her being the brightest and lightest Krishna in the room. Like the improvisation of the metallic lotus flowers, I felt pretty good about this one, as well. As I visualized her as a bigger Krishna, I too, felt myself becoming an even bigger Krishna!

My sales results for the previous week were the best I ever had! Was this a mere coincidence as well? My attitude and assured ease seemed to create a magnetic affect in my life. I thought because of my sales results and recognition, Julie would be ready with her *evil eye.* As Jackson read off the numbers and complimented me on my outstanding results, something unusual happened. Julie was actually smiling and seemed genuinely happy for me. In fact, she congratulated me after the meeting. I remembered the Krishna's warning not to get too emotionally high or low over circumstances. Although I don't actually remember when he taught me this, I just knew the Krishna affirmed this. So, instead of allowing myself to get too excited, or take credit for the change in Julie, I just went inside and felt deep gratitude for my new way of living life. The warmth that was in my heart was indescribable. It was electrifying and quite possibly the most effervescent feeling I had ever experienced.

The rest of the day consisted of different interactions all resulting in manifesting Krishna Kingdoms.

Dream Time

That night as I drifted off to sleep, I was looking forward to being with the Krishna and reviewing my day.

The Krishna sure enough appeared as he had in our previous encounters. He said, "There is much, much more to learn. At this time in your evolvement, before receiving more, you are to work on and gain even more proficiency in these **Three Priceless Techniques.**"

I was evolving, but this required time, process and even mistakes. He said, "There are only two mistakes one can make along the road to truth. Not going all the way and not starting."

I realized I needed time to perfect them. I told him, "I was committed to going all the way!" For a brief moment I felt like he was leaving me, but I quickly realized that he would never do that. He had given me so much, and I needed to repay his kindness by applying these **Three Priceless Techniques.** And, with that, I could swear he gave me one of those smiles of approval and was gone...

The Krishna' Kingdom Challenge

Thank you for reading *Krishna's Kingdom!* We hope you enjoyed the story!

Are you up for a challenge? While you might have trepidation about applying **The Three Priceless Techniques**, as to whether they will work for you; I challenge you to take the **Krishna's Kingdom Challenge!**

It is said that it takes twenty-one days to create a habit. The **Krishna's Kingdom Challenge** is a commitment to practice **The Three Priceless Techniques** for the next twenty-one days. Put them to the test and see how you feel, how much you've progressed on your own *Krishna-scale* and how much your world has improved!

It is also a good idea to read this book, at least once a week each during this time, as you'll most assuredly understand more and experience more.

As you read, the goal is to inspire seven million people to do **The Three Priceless Techniques** consistently. Please let us know that you are committed to this challenge and email us at KrishnasKingdomChallenge@gmail.com. We are here to support you in creating global Krishna Kingdom Meditation Groups.

To further help you to improve your world and the world at large, we highly recommend you do the ***Krishna's Kingdom Blessing Meditation*** daily, which we will be publishing shortly (meanwhile, please meditate and/or do your own prayers daily).

This twenty-two-minute meditation will accelerate your Krishna Nature and help the world to do the same.

Reviews are priceless! Sharing is caring. If you deemed this book valuable, please share your thoughts in an *Amazon* review.

Again, thank you for reading this book. I believe that a picture is worth a thousand words, and an experience is worth a million. While you may want to *tell* others about what you learned, it is better that you *recommend* the book to others; so they may have their own *experience.*

I hope to meet you in a Krishna Kingdom!

Love and Tujechey (Tibetan- May you achieve enlightenment in this incarnation),

Daniel O'Hara and Rekha Balaji

Dedication

I would like to dedicate *Krishna's Kingdom* to my beloved teacher, Maha Atma (meaning Great Soul) Choa Kok Sui. He is as close to a Krishna in the physical form as I have had the pleasure to know. His twenty-two plus years of guidance, blessings, and teachings have given my heart so much joy. He has blessed my family with abundance, has given me the ability to heal others, and given me wisdom to share, improving the lives of others.

I would also like to dedicate this book to the Krishna and Green Tara, whom I believe actually gave me the prompting to write this book. One night in February of 2004, while I was lying in bed and asking for guidance on a business transaction, and in a split-second I was flooded with images of this book. This experience was undeniable, and many of the ideas and events in this book were not in my consciousness until this experience. Who would have thought, that during Super Bowl #38 when the Patriots beat the Panthers, I would have translated these images into this story?

.

Acknowledgements

We'd like to the thank the brilliant Karan Vir and his team at
Vimanika Studios at www.VimanakiaComics.com for creating
our beautiful cover.

    We'd also like to thank Parie Petty at
www.WesternLithographics.com for her support with my books,
Buddha Fields and Christ's Castle.

About The Authors

Daniel O'Hara has lived a unique life, marching to the beat of his own internal drummer. Identifying more in the philosophy of the East, he developed a love of the martial arts at an early age. While searching for martial arts instructors, he realized there was much more to be learned. He then sought out the mystical teachings of the East and found Maha Atma (Great Soul) Choa Kok Sui.

In 1987, at the young age of 19, he left UC Riverside and became a stockbroker. This was during the greed and glory days of Wall Street. He might have been the youngest stockbroker in Dean Witter's illustrious history. He experienced much pain, stress and some success. He became an expert in trading the commodity markets using the vibration of the planets and sacred geometry. This esoteric understanding of how vibration (energy) influences people, further pushed him to understand energy healing.

He has helped bring five companies public and even completed a billion-dollar transaction. He has experienced the highest of highs and the lowest of lows in the world of finance.

After five years in the industry and only in his mid-twenties, he fell apart from stress and looked to rebuild his physical, mental and emotional life. Little did he know at the time that these life lessons would send him on a quest to develop spiritually.

Finding the priceless teachings of Maha Atma Choa, the Modern Founder of Pranic Healing, Daniel was given the tools of self-development, sharing profound wisdom with, and healing others.   Daniel has taught healing seminars in nine states and healed famous professional athletes from the NFL, NBA, MLB and UFC.

Daniel runs the www.OCMeditationGroup.com in Orange County, CA. He is very passionate about many causes including feeding/clothing the impoverished, working for animal rights, promoting sustainability issues and protecting the environment. He has authored *Buddha Fields, Buddha Fields for Addictions and Christ's Castle.*

For more information about Daniel, his meditations and video seminars, please see www.DanielOHara.com, www.ChristCastles.org, and www.ChristParables.com.

Rekha Balaji is an active member of the Orange County Meditation Group over the last four years and has always been drawn towards the spiritual realm since her childhood days. The journey of self-discovery constantly led Rekha to strengthen her belief in the higher powers of the Divine and introduced her into the delightful and invigorating world of metaphysical healing in 2014. She is actively associated with the World Pranic Healing foundation and is certified in basic Pranic Healing and Achieving Oneness with Higher Soul.

In the business world, Rekha is an experienced IT Analyst and is very well versed in the field of financial services where she began her career in 2005. She is always open to exploring new topics of interest and has always had a desire to diversify her work experience in different industry domains. Rekha is currently engaged as an IT Consultant in the insurance domain.

Rekha is aspiring to advance her healing practices in the future. She is very passionate about Bollywood dance, Zumba and music and has been classically trained in Indian music. She is a Bollywood Dance Instructor Trainee with a company based in New York and is looking forward to teaching her passion in the near future.

Rekha in her spare time enjoys supporting charitable organizations alike and donates food and clothing to the homeless through volunteering efforts. She is always receptive to apply all the learnings and teachings of the orange county meditation group led by Daniel O'Hara.

Rekha is very grateful to all the life experiences bestowed to her by the Divine and believes in the power of inner peace and self-love. Her mission is to spread love and light to all sentient beings and help alleviate the sufferings of humanity.